DEAR MOUSE FRIENDS, WELCOME TO THE

STONE AGE!

WELCOME TO THE STONE AGE . . . AND THE WORLD OF THE CAVEMICE!

CAPITAL: OLD MOUSE CITY

POPULATION: WE'RE NOT SURE. (MATH DOESN'T EXIST YET!) BUT BESIDES CAVEMICE, THERE ARE PLENTY OF DINOSAURS, <u>WAY</u> TOO MANY SABER-TOOTHED TIGERS, AND FEROCIOUS CAVE BEARS — BUT NO MOUSE HAS EVER HAD THE COURAGE TO COUNT THEM!

TYPICAL FOOD: PETRIFIED CHEESE SOUP

NATIONAL HOLIDAY: GREAT ZAP DAY, WHICH CELEBRATES THE DISCOVERY OF FIRE. RODENTS EXCHANGE GRILLED CHEESE SANDWICHES ON THIS HOLIDAY.

NATIONAL DRINK: MAMMOTH MILKSHAKES

CLIMATE: Unpredictable, WITH FREQUENT METEOR SHOWERS

cheese soup

milkshake

MONEY

SEASHELLS OF ALL SHAPES AND SIZES

MEASUREMENT

THE BASIC UNIT OF MEASUREMENT IS BASED ON THE LENGTH OF THE TAIL OF THE LEADER OF THE VILLAGE. A UNIT CAN BE DIVIDED INTO A HALF TAIL OR QUARTER TAIL. THE LEADER IS ALWAYS READY TO PRESENT HIS TAIL WHEN THERE IS A DISPUTE.

THE CAVEMICE

Geronimo

Trap

Théa

Benjamin

Bugsy Wugsy

Hercule Poirat

Grandma Ratrock

Geronimo Stilton

CAVEMICE

PAWS OFF
THE PEARL!

Scholastic Inc.

Copyright © 2013 by Edizioni Piemme S.p.A., Palazzo Mondadori, Via Mondadori 1, 20090 Segrate, Italy. International Rights © Atlantyca S.p.A. English translation © 2016 by Atlantyca S.p.A.

The publisher does not have any control over and does not assume any responsibility for author or third-party websites or their content.

GERONIMO STILTON names, characters, and related indicia are copyright, trademark, and exclusive license of Atlantyca S.p.A. All rights reserved. The moral right of the author has been asserted. Based on an original idea by Elisabetta Dami. www.geronimostilton.com

Published by Scholastic Inc., *Publishers since 1920*, 557 Broadway, New York, NY 10012. SCHOLASTIC and associated logos are trademarks and/or registered trademarks of Scholastic Inc.

Stilton is the name of a famous English cheese. It is a registered trademark of the Stilton Cheese Makers' Association. For more information, go to www.stiltoncheese.com.

ISBN 978-1-338-03292-5

Text by Geronimo Stilton
Original title *Trottosauro contro ostrica mannara*
Cover by Flavio Ferron
Illustrations by Giuseppe Facciotto (design) and Alessandro Costa (color)
Graphics by Marta Lorini and Chiara Cebraro

Special thanks to Shannon Penney
Translated by Julia Heim
Interior design by Becky James

10 9 8 7 6 5 4 3 2 1   16 17 18 19 20

Printed in the U.S.A.   40
First printing 2016

MANY AGES AGO, ON PREHISTORIC MOUSE ISLAND, THERE
WAS A VILLAGE CALLED OLD MOUSE CITY. IT WAS INHABITED
BY BRAVE *RODENT SAPIENS* KNOWN AS THE CAVEMICE.
DANGERS SURROUNDED THE MICE AT EVERY TURN:
EARTHQUAKES, METEOR SHOWERS, FEROCIOUS DINOSAURS,
AND FIERCE GANGS OF SABER-TOOTHED TIGERS. BUT THE
BRAVE CAVEMICE FACED IT ALL WITH A SENSE OF HUMOR,
AND WERE ALWAYS READY TO LEND A HAND TO OTHERS.
HOW DO I KNOW THIS? I DISCOVERED AN
ANCIENT BOOK WRITTEN BY MY ANCESTOR, GERONIMO
STILTONOOT! HE CARVED HIS STORIES INTO STONE TABLETS
AND ILLUSTRATED THEM WITH HIS ETCHINGS.
I AM PROUD TO SHARE THESE STONE AGE STORIES WITH
YOU. THE EXCITING ADVENTURES OF THE CAVEMICE WILL
MAKE YOUR FUR STAND ON END, AND THE JOKES WILL
TICKLE YOUR WHISKERS! HAPPY READING!

Geronimo Stilton

WARNING! DON'T IMITATE THE CAVEMICE.
WE'RE NOT IN THE STONE AGE ANYMORE!

GERONIMOOOOO!

It was a calm spring evening in *Old Mouse City*, and I was in a marvemouse mood!

Ah, springtime! Quiet mornings, sun-soaked afternoons, and cool **NIGHTS** filled with stars . . .

Oops — I haven't introduced myself!

My name is Stiltonoot, **GERONIMO STILTONOOT**, and I run *The Stone Gazette*, the most famouse newspaper in prehistory.

Ahhhhh!

As I was saying, spring had arrived in Old Mouse City, and I was full of energy. I had even finished my work at the office early!

Since it was such a **FABUMOUSE** evening, the idea of going right home to my cave didn't seem like much fun. I decided to treat myself to a delicious dinner of Paleolithic cheeses and seasonal vegetables.

Where? At the Rotten Tooth Tavern, of course! That's the restaurant my cousin Trap runs with his business partner, Greasella Stonyfur — a cook so good, she'll make your WHISKERS WOBBLE.

"Geronimo!" Trap hollered when I walked into the tavern. "What a surprise! We were just finishing the last of the **Volcanico cheese quesadillas**."

"Finishing?!" I squeaked.

Volcanico is a special, **SUPER-STINKY** cheese made with sour milk and hot lava peppers. It's rare — and delicious!

Trap gave me a friendly **THUMP** on the back. "Don't worry, we saved some for you! Sit down."

I headed for a table, but before I reached it, I was distracted by a familiar squeak. "Geronimo! Eating alone? Why don't you come over here?"

Gulp — it was the most *fascinating*, extraordinary, FABUMOUSE, **intelligent**, marvemouse, enchanting, *elegant* rodent in not just Old Mouse City, but the entire prehistoric world: *Clarissa* .... *Conjurat!*

Sigh!

For a few moments, I was frozen like a Jurassic GLACIER. Then she said,

"Geronimo? Are you okay?"

"**UMM** . . . no — I mean, y-yes — I mean . . ." I stammered.

Whenever I see Clarissa, my brain turns to **MELTED CHEESY MUSH**!

I sat down across from her, as red as a Paleozoic pepper. But just then —

Gulp!

"WAKE UP!"

The tavern had disappeared. The table had disappeared. And, worst of all, *Clarissa* had disappeared!

It was all just a **dream**!

I looked around, confused. Rat-munching rattlesnakes — I was in my **office** at *The Stone Gazette*!

Great rocky boulders, I must have **Fallen asleep** at my desk! But who woke me?

Huh?

I looked up and saw **Trap** snickering in satisfaction.

"**GOOD MORNING, COUSIN**! Slacking off, I see!" he exclaimed, thumping me on the back so hard that it put my tail in knots.

"What?" I mumbled. "But I worked **all night!**"

Wake up, Cousin!

"**Oh, calm down!** I'm not here to fight." He bent down, looked me square in the eye, and said, "I'm here to give you some **FABUMOUSE** news!"

Massive meteorites! That's not what I wanted to hear. When Trap says he has fabumouse news, it usually means there's about to be **AN AVALANCHE OF TROUBLE!**

LET'S GET GOING!

Trap looked at me with a **smile on his snout.** "I just got a message from Rocky Stonesmith, a friend of mine who lives in

CLEARWATER VILLAGE, the fishing town along the coast."

"Okay," I said. "But what does this have to do with me?"

Trap rolled his eyes. "Give me a minute! Rocky says that they found a GIANT OYSTER in the Clearwater Village lagoon."

I blinked. "SO?"

"Do I have to explain everything to you?" he squeaked with a groan. "A GIANT OYSTER means . . . a giant pearl!"

Wow!

I still didn't understand a cheese crumb of what he was squeaking about!

Trap continued, "Rocky asked for help PULLING the oyster from the lagoon. He and his fellow townsmice can't do it themselves . . ."

"So you volunteered," I finished. "Then what are you still doing here? It sounds like there's no time to lose!"

Trap GRINNED. "Right, there's no time to lose! Because if **we** pull the oyster from the lagoon, Rocky will reward **US**!"

"What do you mean, if **we** pull it out?" I squeaked. "And what do you mean by reward **us**? I'm not going anywhere!"

"ARE YOU SURE?"

Trap said, raising an eyebrow. "Rocky promised to repay me with a bag of **pearls**!"

Fossilized feta! A bag of pearls?

THAT WAS A MOUSERIFIC REWARD!

"It won't be easy for you to get a giant oyster out of the lagoon," I pointed out to my cousin.

But Trap didn't want to hear that. "Trust me, Geronimo! I have a **foolproof** plan!"

"But —"

"**LET'S GET GOING!**" said Trap,

clapping his paws. "It's getting late! Pack your bags, Cousin — we're hitting the road!"

"**NO, NO!**" I said firmly. "I have more important things to do than **DUNK MYSELF** in a lagoon to make you rich."

But Trap wasn't listening. "**GREAT!** So we'll need some things to take along on the trip — one or two extra clubs, and —"

"Trap!" I interrupted. "**I am NOT coming!**"

". . . and two autosauruses, naturally!" he went on, not listening to a word I was squeaking.

"**AUTOSAURUSES?**" I said. "You want to travel by autosaurus?"

"Of course!" he said. "Otherwise, how we will **HAUL** a giant oyster out of the water?"

14

BY THE
GREAT ZAP,

I had a feeling it wasn't going to be easy to **change** my cousin's mind . . .

AREN'T THERE AUTOSAURUSES IN CLEARWATER VILLAGE?

"Do we really need to take **two autosauruses**?" I asked.

Trap nodded. "Absolutely — we need them both to pull the giant pearl out of the water!"

"But aren't there any autosauruses in CLEARWATER VILLAGE?" I asked.

"Nope!" Trap said. "The village's huts are built above the water, raised up on stilts. So the mice don't ride on autosauruses to get around! Instead, they use SKIMMER RAFTS."

Skimmer rafts are used for fishing and **sailing around** the sea. I'd heard

Thea talk about them, but I'd never had the chance to use one. They sounded like fun . . . even though boats always make me **QUEASY**!

"Okay, but can't you ask **SOMEONE ELSE** for help?" I protested.

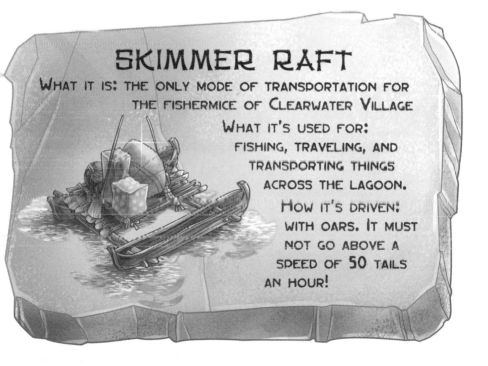

SKIMMER RAFT

WHAT IT IS: THE ONLY MODE OF TRANSPORTATION FOR THE FISHERMICE OF CLEARWATER VILLAGE

WHAT IT'S USED FOR: FISHING, TRAVELING, AND TRANSPORTING THINGS ACROSS THE LAGOON.

HOW IT'S DRIVEN: WITH OARS. IT MUST NOT GO ABOVE A SPEED OF 50 TAILS AN HOUR!

"Don't you understand?" Trap **cried**. "I can't let everyone know that I'm going to haul up a **giant pearl**! It's a super-top-secret mission, and you're the only one I can trust!"

I sighed. He was right — if the citizens of Old Mouse City found out about the huge

The treasure is ours!

Get it! The oyster is ours!

oyster, they'd all run to CLEARWATER YILLAGE to get their  on the pearl first!

"So . . ." I said, shaking in my fur, "wouldn't it be better to just forget it? Some TREASURES are best left alone."

"WHAT ARE YOU SQUEAKING ABOUT?!"

Trap asked.

"WHEN WILL I HAVE ANOTHER CHANCE LIKE THIS??!"

Then he added, "Don't you think that your dear cousin, who has always worked so hard, deserves a REWARD?"

Thundering triceratops! I couldn't believe my ears. Worked hard? The hardest work

Trap did was lie out in the sun and munch on **Volcanico quesadillas**!

"If you really worked hard and didn't take *vacations* six days a week, you would already be rich, Trap!" I said.

He just rolled his eyes. "Come on, **GERONIMO**! You're the only one who can help me. I promise that I'll give at least five — well, three — okay, maybe **HALF** a pearl to *The Stone Gazette*!"

"Gee, **THANKS SO MUCH**!" I snorted. "I think the *Gazette* can do without your **super-generous** offer."

"Hmph," Trap huffed. "You sure are **STONE-HEADED**!"

But before I knew what was happening, he was pushing me out the door of *The Stone Gazette,* calling, "*THEEEEAAAA!*"

A moment later, my sister, Thea, appeared on her autosaurus, **GRUNTY**.

Bones and stones! This was just what I needed!

DIDN'T I TELL YOU?

As soon as Thea climbed off of Grunty, he began to lick me and nibble my tail.

OUCH!
WHaT a PaLEOZOic PaiN!

Then my sister stepped **between** us.

Ouch!

Yum!

"Geronimo, you **Have to Go** with Trap!"

Oh, for the love of cheese!

Thea continued, "This **scoop** is too important

22

to miss! Imagine the article you can chisel about it. Plus, if you don't go and recover the pearl, some **rascally** rodent could steal it for himself!"

"**NO WAY!**" I insisted. "If you think it's so **IMPORTANT**, why don't you go?"

"Oh, of course I'm coming, too, but Grunty is just a baby," Thea responded. "He's *FAST*, but he's not **strong** enough to help pull the giant oyster out of the lagoon."

Out of the corner of my **EYE**, I could see Thea whispering something to Trap. What were those two **plotting**?

Arf!

Arf!

Arf!

23

"But, Trap," said Thea loudly, shooting me a *sneaky* look, "why would Geronimo be interested in a lovely dinner with Clarissa Conjurat?"

Bones and stones! "What does *Clarissa* have to do with any of this?"

Trap shrugged. "**DIDN'T I TELL YOU**? If you come with me, once the **EXPEDITION** is over I'll reserve a **romantic** table for you and Clarissa at the Rotten Tooth Tavern."

"Just imagine it," Thea said. "You and *Clarissa* . . ."

"All alone . . ." added Trap.

Thea sighed. "Lit by **PREHISTORIC CANDLELIGHT** . . ."

"Eating delicious Volcanico cheese . . ." Trap said.

"And at the end of the evening, you

offer Clarissa a necklace of **pearls** from Clearwater Village!" finished Thea.

Petrified cheese! A romantic dinner, just like in my **dream**!

"Well, I guess maybe I could ride to **CLEARWATER VILLAGE** on my autosaurus," I said slowly, "just, you know, to **look** around."

You and Clarissa . . .

All alone!

What?!

"Fabumouse!" Trap cried.

"That's the Geronimo we love — a mouse who's adventurous, courageous, and up for anything!" Thea added, JUMPING up on Grunty.

Adventurous? Courageous? Up for anything?

Ahhh, Clarissa!

WHAT HAD I GOTTEN MYSELF INTO?

YOU CAN'T MISS THIS!

I suddenly felt like *twisting* my tail in knots. I was a goner, doomed, extinct! "On second thought —"

"*YOU CAN'T MISS THIS!*" Trap interrupted.

"You'll never have this chance again!" Thea added.

As much as it ruffled my fur to admit it, they were both right.

Clarissa Conjurat was so FABUMOUSE that a regular rodent like me could never win her **heart**. But if I recovered a giant oyster — and a **giant pearl** — maybe she would notice me!

"Oh, all right," I said with a sigh. "**I'm coming!**"

Thea and Trap exploded in squeaks of joy.

"HOORAY! MOUSETASTIC!"

Right away, Trap found an **autosaurus** who let us load him up in exchange for fresh **snacks** — the most **EFFICIENT** autosaurus fuel!

Thea took Grunty back to his **DEN** to prepare him some food.

But my autosaurus was a total **lazybones** and did not want to leave! To make matters worse, I had no ingredients in my cave for a **Superfruit Smoothie**, my autosaurus's preferred fuel. All I had in my pantry were two **chives** and a dried root. I held those treats out to my autosaurus, but . . .

HE WANTED NOTHING TO DO WITH THEM — OR OUR TRIP!

I climbed on the autosaurus and waved the **chives** under his snout — but he didn't move a millitail!

1

REWARD NO. 1
SOME CHIVES

Then I tried giving him a few **friendly** pats — but he didn't move a millitail!

Finally, I spotted a bowl that I had used for my **super-delicious** dinner of cheese and beans the night before. I let my autosaurus sniff the bowl, then whispered, "As soon as we get back, I promise you a mega-smoothie, SEASONED

THUD

PAT PAT

REWARD NO. 2
SOME FRIENDLY PATS

2

with a pot of cheese and beans!"

With that, my super-lazy autosaurus JUMPED UP and darted out of my cave, faster than a strike of the Great Zap!

Trumpeting triceratops, what a genius idea!

REWARD NO. 3
THE PROMISE OF A MEGA-
SMOOTHIE, SEASONED WITH
CHEESE AND BEANS

CHARGING MAMMOTHS!

Now we just had to get to CLEARWATER VILLAGE, and the autosauruses would take care of the rest! And when we got back to Old Mouse City, my **dream** of impressing Clarissa would finally come true.

"Come on!" I called cheerfully to Trap and Thea. "Let's goooo!"

"I like your attitude!" said Thea, taking a seat behind me on my huge autosaurus.

"Giant oyster, here we come!" Trap added, leading the way on his autosaurus.

After traveling for a few hours under the

scorching sun, we reached the **Rubble River** and decided to take a break. The autosauruses needed some water and rest, and we were all as sweaty as Paleozoic sponges — **YUCK!** — so we took a nice dip in the river.

For a while, we had a fabumouse time **SPLASHiNG** around and jumping off a boulder near the shore.

"WATCH THIS!"

called Trap, jumping into the water and making a splash as tall as a mammoth.

"Now watch me!" I cried, **leaping** into the river with the grace of a swanasaurus.

As Trap and I **swam around** like

prehistoric pike fish, Thea sunbathed on the shore.

Suddenly, the ground began to shake, and Thea jumped to her paws.

Bones and stones, what was going on?

Umm, let's see . . .

Trap and I turned as PALE as Mesozoic mozzarella.

A cloud of dust began to rise **threateningly** in the distance. Then, way up on a small, rocky peak, we could see . . .

Yippee!

a charging mammoth!

ROOOOAAARRRRR!
ROOOAAAAARRRRR!

Fossilized feta, I was shaking in my fur!
Suddenly, **another** mammoth appeared . . .
and then **another** . . . and many, **many
others**!

It was a whole herd of mammoths, and
they were charging at **TOP SPEED**.
It looked like they were running away from
someone — or something!

But the **WORST** part was that the mammoths were headed directly toward Trap and me, and we were FROZEN in fear like two blocks of stone!

There was **no time** to climb ashore, **no time** to swim to the other side, **no time** for anything! Great rocky boulders, we were finished — done for — extinct!

EXTINCTION!

Trap and I finally got our tails in gear and started swimming. In our **panic**, we didn't realize that we were swimming against the current — so we hadn't moved a **millitail**!

Now the herd was stomping into the water, making huge waves!

SPLISH! SPLASH! SPLOSH!

To make matter worse, Thea had **disappeared**. Fossilized feta, what if she had been trampled?

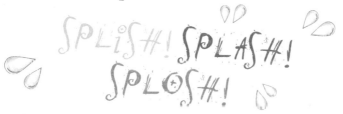

SPLISH! SPLASH! SPLOSH!

The mammoths were thumping closer and closer.

Trap and I squeezed our **EYES** shut and prepared for the worst, when . . .

"Geronimo! Trap! **OVER HERE!**"

Bones and stones — it was Thea!

She stood on top of a nearby boulder,

getting ready to throw an **enoRMouSe** vine lasso out to us.

"**WE'RE READY, THEA!**" I squeaked.

Thea tossed the vine — and reached us on her first try!

We grabbed on, Thea and the autosauruses pulled the vine, and we were **HAULED** out of the way just before the **MaMMotHs** would have trampled us. Whew!

"We're saved!" I squeaked, my whiskers still wobbling in fright.

42

Trap and I watched as the mammoths reached the other side of the river and continued stampeding, **TRUMPETING**, and **huffing**.

How strange! Usually mammoths are **peaceful** creatures. Why were they acting so crazy? What could have frightened them?

Soaking wet, we hugged my super-tough SISTER.

"Thanks, Thea!" I exclaimed. "If it weren't for you, Trap and I would have been **mouse pancakes**!"

MOVE IT, GERONIMO!

There was no time to waste — we had to get back on the road to Clearwater Village!

We left the **Rubble River** and rode our autosauruses into a thick forest. But before long, I couldn't shake the feeling that someone was hiding in the trees . . . **WATCHING US**.

I mentioned it to Thea and Trap, but they both just **ROLLED** their eyes.

"Oh, don't be such a scaredy-mouse, Geronimo!" Trap scoffed.

As we slowly continued through the **WOODS**, I thought I heard some strange sounds, too, such as . . .

Stifled laughter: **HEE, HEE, HEE!**
Teeth chattering: **Cha-cha-cha!**
Nails scratching:

SCRATCH! SCRATCH! SCRATCH!

A **HORRIBLE THOUGHT** scampered through my mind: What if there were SABER-TOOTHED TIGERS hiding in the forest?

Squeak! How terrifying!

"Don't you hear that?" I asked as I looked *TO THE RIGHT* ➡ and ⬅ *TO THE LEFT*.

"There's no one here," Thea said calmly.

"You always think everything is so **FUR-RAISING**," Trap added with a wink.

But I was sure we weren't alone — and now I could smell something, too. It was the unmistakable **STINK** of moldy wild fur!

I was so busy sniffing the air that I banged my head right into a tree. **Whack!**

Then a branch slapped me square in the snout. **YOUCH!**

I lost my balance and fell right on top of

a nest of **jumping ants** — the most dangerous insects in all of prehistory! Petrified cheese, what had I gotten myself into?

"MOVE, GERONIMO, OR THEY'LL BITE YOU!"

Thea yelled from her autosaurus.

"But they're so fast!" I squeaked.

The ants were already jumping up and pricking, NIBBLING, and biting my tail with their super-SHARP little teeth.

OUCHIE!

Bones and stones, these ants were hungrier than a **T. REX** at dinnertime!

CHOMP CHOMP CHOMP!

I had to get out of there! I glanced over

at Thea and my **autosaurus**, but —
bouncing boulders, where were they?

By now, the **ants** were everywhere. They
were even jumping off the trees, with their
jaws **WIDE** open and their **TINY FANGS**
in plain sight!

I began to run as fast as I could, but just

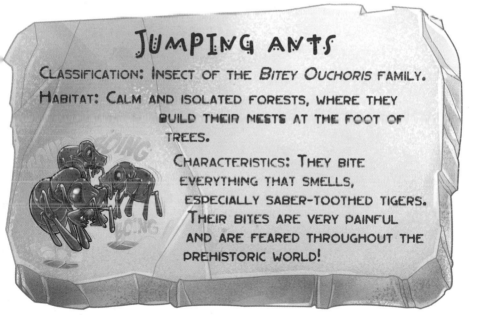

JUMPING ANTS

CLASSIFICATION: INSECT OF THE *BITEY OUCHORIS* FAMILY.

HABITAT: CALM AND ISOLATED FORESTS, WHERE THEY
BUILD THEIR NESTS AT THE FOOT OF
TREES.

CHARACTERISTICS: THEY BITE
EVERYTHING THAT SMELLS,
ESPECIALLY SABER-TOOTHED TIGERS.
THEIR BITES ARE VERY PAINFUL
AND ARE FEARED THROUGHOUT THE
PREHISTORIC WORLD!

as I really got going, I **TRIPPED** on a root. Oh, what a day!

Before I knew it, the **ants** had surrounded me in attack formation. They weren't

just **FAST**, they were also extremely organized — and ready to finish me off by unleashing their fangs on my tail!

GOOD-BYE, PREHISTORIC WORLD!

SNIFF, SNIFF, SNIFF!

I was as dazed as a dizzy dinosaur, as immobile as a MAMMOTH SKELETON, and as petrified as a FOSSIL!

But just when I was ready to give up, something incredible happened.

The jumping ants suddenly began to sniff the air . . .

Boing!

Boing!

Boing!

SNIFF SNIFF SNIFF

SNIFF SNIFF

SNIFF, SNIFF, SNIFF!

Wait a minute . . .

Were they sniffing **ME**?

I had just taken a *shower* one month earlier — I was hardly smelly at all!

Continuing to sniff, the ants jumped away and disappeared into the **SHRUBS**.

I was left lying on the ground, stiff and stinging. I was expecting the ants to **come back** at any moment — but they didn't. **WHEW!**

They must have found something more interesting to nibble on! But there was no one else around . . . or was there?

"Move it, Geronimo! What are you waiting for?" Thea squeaked, popping out of the

forest on my **autosaurus**.

As soon as I climbed up, I caught a whiff of the **stink** that I had smelled earlier.

"Do you smell it now?" I said.

"Smell what?" Thea said.

I wrinkled my snout. "That awful prehistoric **STENCH**!"

Jump on!

?!

Thea and Trap both shook their snouts. They didn't smell a thing!

"I think it's the horrific smell of a **SABER-TOOTHED TIGER**!" I cried.

"What are you squeaking about, you megalithic worrywart?" asked Trap. "What kind of **TIGERS** would be in a place like this?"

But Thea looked thoughtful. "Well, it's true that **jumping ants'** favorite food is saber-toothed tiger," she said. "Keep your **EYES** open and snouts up. Geronimo could be right!"

Before long, a **FUR-RAISING** scream echoed through the forest.

Massive meteorites, what was that?

"**AAAAAAAAAAAAAAH!**"

There was no doubt about it — that was a feline screech!

Just a few tails away from us, three (**YES, THREE!**) enormouse saber-toothed tigers leaped out of the woods as if they had been **PRICKED** by a hundred Paleozoic pins!

The fanged felines jumped and clawed at their fur, trying to get those terrible ants off of them.

"**GROWWWWL!** That itches!"

"**Roarrr!** That hurts!"

"**Meooooow!** Owwwww!"

"Serves you right, you crusty cats!" Trap declared, waving a paw. "Go **de-bug**

yourselves somewhere else! **SHOO!**"

For once, the tigers didn't have time to **ATTACK US**! Who would have thought that those terrible jumping **ants** would save our fur?

But there was one thing I still didn't understand — what were three ferocious saber-toothed tigers doing on the road to **CLEARWATER VILLAGE**?

HEAVE-HO!

Once we made it past the jumping ants, the rest of our trip to Clearwater Village was **easy cheesy**.

The village sat on a bay, sheltered from the wind and the waves of the ocean. The houses were suspended on WOODEN stilts over the clear water of the lagoon. Everything was so beautiful and clean . . . except for the heaps of **rotten** algae everywhere!

Great rocky Boulders, it StUNK!

"What do the mice of Clearwater Village do with all this **stinky algae**?" I wondered.

Rocky

Just then, Trap's friend **ROCKY** arrived. "Welcome to Clearwater Village, friends!" he greeted us.

"Hey there, Rocky!" Trap called. "We're here to help with the giant pearl!"

Rocky led us over to the shore, where a fleet of skimmer rafts was ready to take us out to the **heart** of the lagoon.

Anytime I have to board a boat, I'm usually a teeny-tiny bit scared. But the water was so calm, and my SKIMMER

RAFT looked so sturdy. I felt safe — and not even the littlest bit SEASICK! It was a megalithic miracle!

Trap's autosaurus followed us, stomping through the shallow water, while mine stayed on the shore. When we ARRIVED by the giant oyster, the skimmer rafts stopped.

"First," Trap said, pulling a rope out of his bag, "we need to tie this rope around the oyster."

The fishermice immediately DOVE into the water with the rope.

"FABUMOUSE!" said Trap. "The hardest part is done. Now the rest is up to you, Geronimo!"

"Me?!" I squeaked. "What am I supposed do?"

Trap winked and explained what he had in mind.

Then Rocky and his **friends** headed back to shore with me, towing the end of the rope. On shore, I tied the rope to my autosaurus and **JUMPED** on his back. We were ready!

Out in the middle of the lagoon, Trap's autosaurus began to *PUSH* the giant oyster with his snout, while my autosaurus *PULLED* the oyster from the shore.

HEAVE-HO!

"It's starting to move!" Thea cried.

GREAT ROCKY BOULDERS — THIS WAS A RATTASTIC IDEA!

The plan was *working* perfectly! Once the oyster was safely out of the water,

Rocky and the others carefully *tickled* it to open it up.

Tickle … tickle … tickle …

When the shell finally opened, we were **BLINDED** by a brilliant light.

FOSSILIZED FETA, WHAT A SPECTACULAR SIGHT!

That's good!

SO WE MEET AGAIN!

It was one of the most amazing moments in prehistory!

We could see that the pearl inside the shell was enormouse, perfectly round, and marvemousely sparkly.

"Mission accomplished!" Rocky rejoiced.

"HOORAY FOR THE STILTONOOTS!" everyone cried, jumping for joy.

But just then . . .

ROOOOAAAAR!

A horrible roar made our whiskers tremble and our fur stand on end. We all spun around, ready to protect our tails.

We were really in **hot lava** now!

Striped **FUR**, pointy **FANGS**, angry **EYES**, super-sharp **CLAWS** — it was **TIGER KHAN**, the ferocious leader of the saber-toothed tigers!

Our fishermice friends were as petrified as hunks of **GRANITE**!

After all, the mice of Clearwater Village are peaceful. Their city is protected by the water on one side and **jumping ants** on the other, so they never expect to see **SABER-TOOTHED TIGERS** storm in!

Tiger Khan took a step toward us, followed by three **BANDAGED** tigers. Those were

the same fearsome felines we'd seen in the **FOREST** earlier!

Bones and stones — they had **followed** us all the way to Clearwater Village!

"**SO WE MEET AGAIN!**" Tiger Khan snarled. "My henchcats have done an excellent job tracking down the **giant**

We want the pearl!

pearl of Clearwater Village."

Rocky stepped in front of the pearl, ready to protect it.

Shaking in our fur, Thea, Trap, and I followed his lead. We weren't about to let a mangy feline get his paws on the pearl!

Tiger Khan HISSED, "If you cooperate, I won't tear out a single one of your WHiSKeRS."

I gulped.

"But if one of you **DARES** to fight back," he added wickedly, licking his lips, "you will be served on a **PLATTER** at my table this evening, with Paleozoic onions and Jurassic potatoes as a side dish!"

Yikes! No one squeaked a single word.

We outnumbered the four tigers, but the rodents of Clearwater Village were no help. They were scared squeakless! What could we do? The giant pearl was in **DANGER** — and we were one step from extinction!

GOOD-BYE, PREHISTORIC WORLD!

FIRE!

Combing his long claws through his **FUR**, Tiger Khan ordered his henchcats, "Get moving!"

The three tigers jumped to attention. **Quick** as arrows, they darted to gather strips of wood and construct a stretcher for carrying the pearl back to their home in Bugville.

We watched helplessly as one tiger tried to lift the giant pearl onto the stretcher — but it was **Megalithically heavy**!

"Careful, you **fearsome fuzzball**!" Tiger Khan snapped. "If something happens to the pearl, I'll make sure those jumping ants know exactly where to find you!"

"Y-y-yes, of course!" the tiger stuttered, trying not to lose his balance.

Holey prehistoric cheese, was this the end

of the magnificent pearl?

Meanwhile, sneaky as a rat, Rocky had assembled some fishermice up on the stilt houses. Now he was whispering something to them.

A moment later . . .

"FIRE, FISHERMICE!"

Rocky yelled so loudly that my fur stood on end. "Paws off the pearl, tigers!"

The mice darted into their huts and came out armed with STRANGE CONTRAPTIONS . . . wooden catapults!

The fishermice loaded the catapults with heaps and heaps of the rotten algae we had seen piled around the village.

YUCK!

The **CATAPULTS** had fabumouse aim, so before they knew what hit their feline fur, the tigers were covered in algae. It was **REALLY** slimy, **REALLY** stinky, and really, REALLY, **really** itchy!

"HOW STINKY!"
"How painful!"
"How itchy!"

Now that they were stinky, in pain, and had a megalithic itch to scratch, the ferocious saber-toothed tigers scampered around like frightened kittens.

"This algae from the lagoon is our secret weapon!" Rocky explained to us, winking. "Since Clearwater Village's only natural DEFENSES are the sea and the jumping ants, we always make sure to have a backup plan."

"The catapults are fabumouse," Thea said in admiration.

"Not to mention that algae," Trap added, plugging his snout. "PEE-YEW!"

The tigers had been forced to retreat from the rain of rotten algae. They'd scurried off after their leader, meowing and mangy.

The air was **megalithically stinky**, but the rotten algae smell was still better than being surrounded by Tiger Khan and his fanged gang!

A MARVEMOUSE DISCOVERY!

When the felines **DISAPPEARED** from sight, we all breathed a great sigh of relief. Massive meteorites, that was a close call! But I didn't feel calm . . .

"What happened today could happen again!" I worried.

"Geronimo is right," Thea said. "The **giant pearl** is still in danger. Tiger Khan won't give up such a precious treasure without a **fight**!"

Trap elbowed me and whispered, "Listen, Geronimo, I thought that maybe . . . how can I say this? Well . . ."

"What is it, Trap?" I asked.

But he clapped a paw over my mouth.

"Shhhh! I don't want them to hear!"

Then Trap whispered, so quietly I could barely hear, "I think that maybe the giant pearl should **STAY** where it was."

"**HUH?**" What in the Stone Age was my cousin squeaking about?

"I know, I know!" he added. "It would be a terrible waste — that **PRECⁱoUS** jewel, down there in the mud. But the pearl would be much **SAFER** back inside the oyster . . ."

I couldn't believe my ears! Trap, the **greediest** rodent in all of prehistory, was trying to **PR⊙+ECt** a natural treasure?!

"Trap!" I exclaimed. "I'm so **proud** of you!"

Thea, who had been listening, announced loudly, "Friends of Clearwater Village, Trap just had a **marvemouse** idea — we'll return the pearl to its natural habitat!"

"But then no one can **ADMIRE IT**!" one fishermouse said.

"And someone could secretly try to **dig** it up again," another added.

"Wait, **I'VE GOT IT**!" Rocky interrupted, clapping his paws in triumph. "We can return the oyster and **pearl** to the water, and everyone will still be able to see it — because we'll surround it with transparent walls in the middle of the **lagoon!**"

Pointy triceratops horns, what was he squeaking about?

"Did you say TRANSPARENT WALLS?" I asked. "How is that possible?"

"Come with me," Rocky said, waving a paw.

He led us to the Cave of Crabs, a small cavern nestled in a **ROCK** wall near the lagoon. There, Rocky told us a truly **incredible** story!

"The fishermice seek shelter in this cave when it **RAINS**," he explained. "Once, when I was here with my friends, we decided to light a **FIRE**. But since we didn't have any wood, we **SCRATCHED** a strange, white, salty **mold** off the walls of the cave and tried to **burn it**. To our surprise, the fire lit! But as it was burning, the mold fused with the **sand** on the ground and formed a strange mixture. Once it was **cold**, the mixture turned into a **TRANSPARENT** sheet."

Thea, Trap, and I listened to Rocky's story, **fascinated**.

WE SCRATCHED A STRANGE, WHITE, SALTY MOLD OFF THE WALLS . . .

WE TRIED TO BURN IT, AND THE FIRE LIT!

THE MOLD FUSED WITH THE SAND AND FORMED A STRANGE MIXTURE . . .

"We called it GLAZITE!" Rocky concluded. "We worked with it and learned to make it THIN and transparent, almost like air. We did many experiments — and here's the result!"

BY THE GREAT ZAP!

Our mouths fell open. In the cave were not **one**, not **two**, not **THREE**, but

TONS of transparent sheets in all shapes and sizes!

"Thundering triceratops!" I exclaimed. "This is a marvemouse discovery!"

I examined the whitish MOLD that grew on the walls of the cave. It was truly mouserific!

Then I closed my eyes and let my **imagination** run wild, like a rat with a saber-toothed tiger on his tail. I could think of a million things to build using GLAZITE!

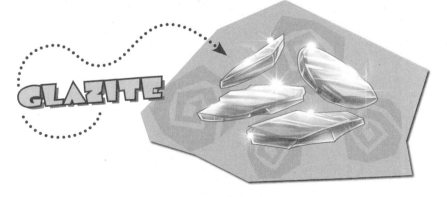

It would allow us to keep **warmth** and sound inside a cave or hut but still see outside!

For all the bones in a dinosaur, one thing was certain — thanks to the glazite, our lives as **CAVEMICE** could get so much better!

WHAT A SIGHT!

The next day, the village was buzzing. All the townsmice were working their paws to the bone to bring Rocky's idea to life.

Thea, Trap, and I were busy, too! With the

There you go!

Come on!

help of our **autosauruses**, we had put the giant pearl back in the center of the **lagoon**. We positioned it right inside the open oyster.

Rocky and the others carried TREE TRUNKS on their skimmer rafts, and used them to build a WOODEN structure around the oyster.

"Now that the **STRUCTURE** is ready," Rocky

Bang! Bang! Bang!

Heave-ho!

said, "we can put up the TRANSPARENT WALLS!"

The townsmice scampered around, loading the sheets of glazite onto their skimmer rafts and securing them to the wooden posts.

Holey cheese — we could see the open oyster perfectly through the glazite!

"Now the pearl is SAFE," said Trap, satisfied.

When the work was finally finished, the mice of Clearwater Village organized an ENORMOUSE PARTY! There was a huge banquet with tons of Paleozoic cheese tarts, rolls of spicy algae, and Mammoth milkshakes.

CHOMP CHOMP CHOMP CHOMP CHOMP

"Delicious!" Trap mumbled around a mouthful of a dozen Paleozoic CHEESE tarts.

Rocky got to his paws and gave a fabumouse speech, thanking us for our help and presenting us with a reward from the village mice.

When Rocky waved the pouch full of PRECiOUS Clearwater Village pearls that he was giving us under Trap's WHiSKeRS, my cousin gasped — and a tart almost went down the wrong way!

GULP! COUGH!

I was happy, but not just because of the precious pearls we were paid. Our trip had also given us the gift of glazite, a discovery that would completely transform the way we cavemice lived.

I couldn't wait to return to *Old Mouse City* and tell everyone there about our mouserific adventure!

I had to write an **article** for the next edition of *The Stone Gazette* right away. Bones and stones — I would etch an

Gulp!

Here they are!

entire SPECIAL EDITION dedicated to the sensational discovery!

I could already picture the headline: **Glazite: A Discovery for the Prehistoric Record Books!**

AREN'T YOU FORGETTING SOMETHING?

Before we knew it, it was time for us to **return** to Old Mouse City.

After saying good-bye to Rocky and our new friends from **CLEARWATER VILLAGE**, we headed home on our autosauruses. For once, we didn't run into any surprises, so we arrived in *Old Mouse City* before sunset.

When we got back to my cave, Trap, Thea, and I divided the **pearls** from Rocky into three equal piles.

"Thanks for convincing

me to go," I said sheepishly. "That really was a mousetastic **ADVENTURE**! Now I'm ready for bed, though — I'm so tired, I could sleep through a saber-toothed tiger attack."

But Trap held up a paw.

"Aren't you **FORGETTING** something?" he asked, making himself a **MaMMOtH MiLKSHaKe** (out of my ingredients!).

"**What?**" I muttered, confused.

"Don't you remember?" said Thea with a grin. "The **DiNNeR**!"

"But we ate like megalosauruses at Rocky's party . . ." I protested.

RAT-MUNCHING

Aren't you forgetting something?

99

RATTLESNAKES! I suddenly remembered what they were squeaking about!

Between the pearls, the discovery of GLAZITE, and the party, I had completely forgotten about my evening with Clarissa Conjurat!

"You aren't thinking of **backing out**, are you?" Thea asked.

I imagined it: Clarissa and me, sitting together . . .

Gulp! HOW EMBARRASSING! Just the thought made my whiskers wobble, and my heart started beating like the gong of Ernest Heftymouse, our village leader!

"**Maybe it would be better to reschedule,**

Clarissa

y-y-you know," I stammered. "I have a t-t-ton of things to do, and —"

"Oh yeah, like what?" Trap pressed, standing **SNOUT TO SNOUT** with me.

"Well, uh, I have to etch the special edition of *The Stone Gazette* dedicated to the discovery of **GLAZITE**."

"You can do that tomorrow!" Thea pointed out.

"But . . . I also have to explain to our **inventor**, Leo Edistone, how the townspeople of Clearwater Village make glazite from **MOLD**!" I squeaked.

"Oh, you scaredy-mouse!" Trap cried. "Those things can all happen tomorrow, and you know it."

THEA agreed. "Enough nonsense, Geronimo! I'll help you get ready. You need to look **FABUMOUSE** for such a special occasion." She gave me a once-over from head to tail. "Your outfit is all **stained** and **wrinkled**."

I glanced down. After that trip to Clearwater Village, I was definitely looking worse for the wear. And after the avalanche of rotten algae, I **smelled** worse than rancid ricotta!

What a **MEGALITHIC MESS**!

Forget the romantic dinner — if she saw me like this, Clarissa would **scamper off** with her paws up! I needed Thea's help, and fast.

"Calm down, Geronimo," she reassured me. "I'll make you look like a true **gentlemouse** in no time!"

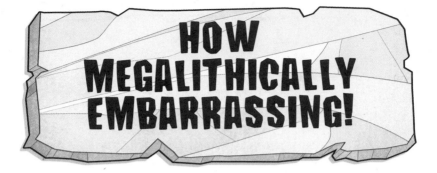

HOW MEGALITHICALLY EMBARRASSING!

First, Thea decided that I had to etch a fancy dinner invitation for Clarissa.

Purple with embarrassment, I got a stone out and began to etch: *Marvemouse Clarissa, would you do me the honor of dining with me one of these evenings? Maybe* **this evening**? *Or, if you'd like, tomorrow evening? But if you're busy, please don't worry about it —* "Geronimo!"

Thea reprimanded, glancing at the

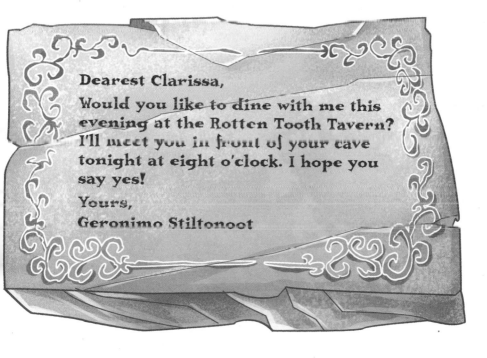

invitation over my shoulder. "What in prehistory are you etching?"

She threw out my invitation and forced me to etch what she dictated, **word for word**.

Fossilized feta, there was no way out!

Here's what it ended up looking like:

Dearest Clarissa,

Would you like to dine with me this evening at the Rotten Tooth Tavern? I'll meet you in front of your cave tonight at eight o'clock. I hope you say yes!

Yours,

Geronimo Stiltonoot

A FULL BATH, WITH SOAP UP TO MY WHISKERS

1

2

FUR TREATMENT

As soon as the invitation was ready, we passed it to a **MAIL-A-DACTYL** so that it would reach *Clarissa* quickly.

How megalithically **embarrassing**!

But that wasn't the end of it. Thea forced me to take a bath, complete with soap up to my whiskers (even though my last bath, a month ago, had plenty of suds!).

Then she *groomed* me and combed my fur . . . **2**

And she poured an entire bowl of prehistoric musk *cologne* on me! **3**

PREHISTORIC MUSK COLOGNE

She even dressed me up in a formal **SUIT**. **4**

Finally, she placed the bag of **pearls** in my paw and sent me off to Clarissa's cave.

"But, I'm not ready," I protested.

Thea **shook her snout**. "I don't want to hear ANOTHER WORD, Geronimo. This is a once-in-a-lifetime opportunity!"

A FORMAL SUIT

"I-I —" I stammered.

"Don't ruffle my fur!" Thea said, waving her **CLUB** in front of my face.

Gasp! I knew I'd better do what she said!

I had no choice but to leave my cave.

To my surprise, Clarissa was already waiting for me at the door of her cave — and she looked *so elegant*. The thought that she had gotten dressed up just to go out with me made my whiskers *wobble*!

BONES AND STONES, I FELT LIKE I MIGHT FAINT AT ANY MOMENT!

"Hi, Geronimo!" Clarissa greeted me. "You were very sweet to invite me to dinner."

S-s-sweet? Pointy triceratops horns, Clarissa had just told me that I was *sweet*!

I turned red from the ends of my ears to the tip of my tail.

"Umm, it's my **p-p-pleasure!**" I responded. Then I gave her my arm, and **together** we headed to the Rotten Tooth Tavern. I felt like the luckiest rodent in prehistory!

When we reached the TAVERN, Trap had reserved a romantic table for us, with lots of

Umm . . .

flaming torches and a bouquet of Paleolithic flowers!

My paws finally stopped shaking, and I told Clarissa all about the **ADVENTURE** I'd just been on. When it was time for dessert, I gave her the bag of pearls.

"Ooooh, Geronimo!" she cried in delight, stunned. "They're beautiful!" And before I knew what was happening, she gave me a kiss right on the tip of my snout!

It's still hard for me to believe, but, thanks to Thea and Trap, the dream that I'd had at the beginning of this adventure had become a reality! By the Great Zap — anything was possible!

After that, you can bet I'll be on the lookout for my next adventure in the Stone Age, or I'm not . . .

Geronimo Stiltonoot, cavemouse!

Don't miss any adventures of the cavemice!

#1 The Stone of Fire

#2 Watch Your Tail!

#3 Help, I'm in Hot Lava!

#4 The Fast and the Frozen

#5 The Great Mouse Race

#6 Don't Wake the Dinosaur!

#7 I'm a Scaredy-Mouse!

#8 Surfing for Secrets

#9 Get the Scoop, Geronimo!

#10 My Autosaurus Will Win!

#11 Sea Monster Surprise

#12 Paws Off the Pearl!

Up Next!

#13 The Smelly Search

Be sure to read all my fabumouse adventures!

#1 Lost Treasure of the Emerald Eye

#2 The Curse of the Cheese Pyramid

#3 Cat and Mouse in a Haunted House

#4 I'm Too Fond of My Fur!

#5 Four Mice Deep in the Jungle

#6 Paws Off, Cheddarface!

#7 Red Pizzas for a Blue Count

#8 Attack of the Bandit Cats

#9 A Fabumouse Vacation for Geronimo

#10 All Because of a Cup of Coffee

#11 It's Halloween, You 'Fraidy Mouse!

#12 Merry Christmas, Geronimo!

#13 The Phantom of the Subway

#14 The Temple of the Ruby of Fire

#15 The Mona Mousa Code

#16 A Cheese-Colored Camper

#17 Watch Your Whiskers, Stilton!

#18 Shipwreck on the Pirate Islands

#19 My Name Is Stilton, Geronimo Stilton

#20 Surf's Up, Geronimo!

#21 The Wild, Wild West

#22 The Secret of Cacklefur Castle

A Christmas Tale

#23 Valentine's Day
Disaster

#24 Field Trip to
Niagara Falls

#25 The Search for
Sunken Treasure

#26 The Mummy
with No Name

#27 The Christmas
Toy Factory

#28 Wedding
Crasher

#29 Down and Out
Down Under

#30 The Mouse Island
Marathon

#31 The Mysterious
Cheese Thief

Christmas Catastrophe

#32 Valley of the
Giant Skeletons

#33 Geronimo and the
Gold Medal Mystery

#34 Geronimo Stilton,
Secret Agent

#35 A Very Merry
Christmas

#36 Geronimo's
Valentine

#37 The Race Across
America

#38 A Fabumouse
School Adventure

#39 Singing Sensation

#40 The Karate Mouse

#41 Mighty Mount
Kilimanjaro

#42 The Peculiar
Pumpkin Thief

#43 I'm Not a
Supermouse!

#44 The Giant
Diamond Robbery

#45 Save the White
Whale!

#46 The Haunted
Castle

#47 Run for the Hills, Geronimo!

#48 The Mystery in Venice

#49 The Way of the Samurai

#50 This Hotel Is Haunted!

#51 The Enormouse Pearl Heist

#52 Mouse in Space!

#53 Rumble in the Jungle

#54 Get Into Gear, Stilton!

#55 The Golden Statue Plot

#56 Flight of the Red Bandit

The Hunt for the Golden Book

#57 The Stinky Cheese Vacation

#58 The Super Chef Contest

#59 Welcome to Moldy Manor

The Hunt for the Curious Cheese

#60 The Treasure of Easter Island

#61 Mouse House Hunter

#62 Mouse Overboard!

The Hunt for the Secret Papyrus

#63 The Cheese Experiment

#64 Magical Mission

#65 Bollywood Burglary

The Hunt for the Hundredth Key

Join me and my friends as we travel through time in these very special editions!

THE JOURNEY THROUGH TIME

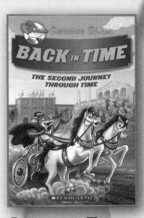

BACK IN TIME:
THE SECOND JOURNEY THROUGH TIME

THE RACE AGAINST TIME:
THE THIRD JOURNEY THROUGH TIME

LOST IN TIME:
THE FOURTH JOURNEY THROUGH TIME

MEET
Geronimo Stiltonord

He is a mouseking — the Geronimo Stilton of the ancient far north! He lives with his brawny and brave clan in the village of Mouseborg. From sailing frozen waters to facing fiery dragons, every day is an adventure for the micekings!

#1 Attack of the Dragons

#2 The Famouse Fjord Race

#3 Pull the Dragon's Tooth!

#4 Stay Strong, Geronimo!

Don't miss any of my adventures in the Kingdom of Fantasy!

THE KINGDOM OF FANTASY

THE QUEST FOR PARADISE:
THE RETURN TO THE KINGDOM OF FANTASY

THE AMAZING VOYAGE:
THE THIRD ADVENTURE IN THE KINGDOM OF FANTASY

THE DRAGON PROPHECY:
THE FOURTH ADVENTURE IN THE KINGDOM OF FANTASY

THE VOLCANO OF FIRE:
THE FIFTH ADVENTURE IN THE KINGDOM OF FANTASY

THE SEARCH FOR TREASURE:
THE SIXTH ADVENTURE IN THE KINGDOM OF FANTASY

THE ENCHANTED CHARMS:
THE SEVENTH ADVENTURE IN THE KINGDOM OF FANTASY

THE PHOENIX OF DESTINY:
AN EPIC KINGDOM OF FANTASY ADVENTURE

THE HOUR OF MAGIC:
THE EIGHTH ADVENTURE IN THE KINGDOM OF FANTASY

THE WIZARD'S WAND:
THE NINTH ADVENTURE IN THE KINGDOM OF FANTASY

MEET
GERONIMO STILTONIX

He is a spacemouse — the Geronimo Stilton of a parallel universe! He is captain of the spaceship *MouseStar 1*. While flying through the cosmos, he visits distant planets and meets crazy aliens. His adventures are out of this world!

#1 Alien Escape

#2 You're Mine, Captain!

#3 Ice Planet Adventure

#4 The Galactic Goal

#5 Rescue Rebellion

#6 The Underwater Planet

#7 Beware! Space Junk!

#8 Away in a Star Sled

#9 Slurp Monster Showdown

#10 Pirate Spacecat Attack

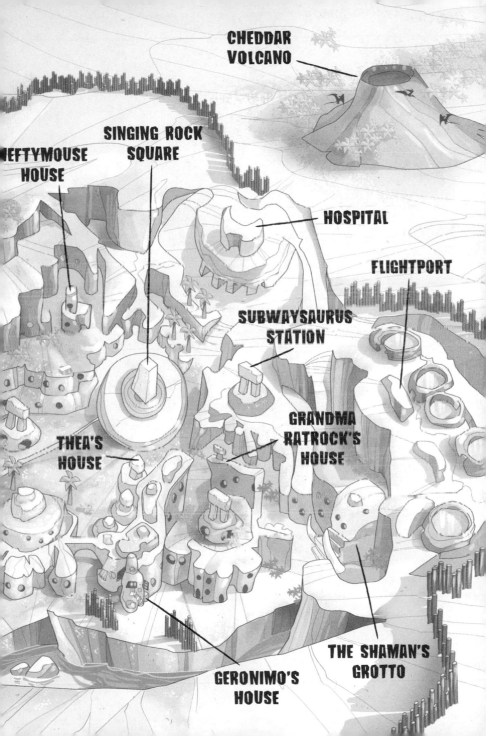

CHEDDAR VOLCANO

SINGING ROCK SQUARE

EFTYMOUSE HOUSE

HOSPITAL

FLIGHTPORT

SUBWAYSAURUS STATION

THEA'S HOUSE

GRANDMA RATROCK'S HOUSE

GERONIMO'S HOUSE

THE SHAMAN'S GROTTO

DEAR MOUSE FRIENDS,

THANKS FOR READING,

AND GOOD-BYE UNTIL

THE NEXT BOOK!